ZAC POWER

D1316217

hardie grant EGMONT

Fossil Fury
published in 2013 by
Hardie Grant Egmont
Ground Floor, Building 1, 658 Church Street
Richmond, Victoria 3121, Australia
www.hardiegrantegmont.com.au

A CiP record for this title is available from the National Library of Australia.

Cover and Illustrations by Craig Phillips
Cover design by Simon Swingler

Printed in Australia by Griffin Press, an Accredited ISO AS/NZS
14001:2004 Environmental Management System printer.

3 5 7 9 10 8 6 4 2

The paper this book is printed on is certified against the
Forest Stewardship Council® Standards. Griffin Press holds
FSC chain of custody certification SGS-COC-005088. FSC
promotes environmentally responsible, socially beneficial
and economically viable management of the world's forests.

FOSSIL FURY
BY H.I. LARRY

ILLUSTRATIONS BY CRAIG PHILLIPS

hardie grant EGMONT

CHAPTER 1

'Zac, could you please carry this bag of manure?'

Zac Power and his mum were at the garden centre. It wasn't the sort of place you'd expect to find a top-secret spy. But that's exactly what Zac was.

Zac's whole family worked for an elite spy agency called the Government

Investigation Bureau, or GIB for short.

Being a spy was supposed to be cool. The last time Zac checked, carrying a bag of manure was not cool – especially when you were wearing your brand new Axe Grinder T-shirt!

'Yuck!' said Zac. 'Do I have to?'

'Yes,' said his mum. You could tell from the look on her face why her secret spy name was Agent Bum Smack. 'I'm carrying all these pot plants. Actually, that reminds me – it's your turn to take out the compost when we get home.'

Zac groaned. The compost smelled even worse than manure! He picked up the heavy plastic bag of Grundy's Garden

Grower and followed his mum out to the car park.

Zac's nose twitched as he walked outside. He could smell something. Not the manure ... something good. There was a sausage sizzle in the car park!

Sweet, thought Zac. *I've earned a snack.*

'I'm just going to get a sausage,' he told his mum, once he'd dumped the manure in the car boot.

As Zac walked over to the sausage sizzle, he noticed something strange. The guy flipping the sausages was staring right at him.

Zac's spy senses tingled. He didn't recognise the man at all, but the man sure seemed to recognise him.

'Hello,' said the man, handing Zac a sausage in bread. 'Why don't you help yourself to some extra-spicy chilli mustard sauce? It's your favourite, isn't it?'

Zac raised an eyebrow and nodded. How did the man know?

Zac reached for the plastic bottle on the table and held it over the sausage in bread. But when he squeezed the bottle, nothing came out.

'Hey, it's empty!' Zac said.

'Try again,' said the man, winking at him.

Zac frowned and gave the bottle a shake. Something rattled inside it.

He glanced around to make sure no-one was looking, and then twisted the lid off. He tipped the contents into his hand.

All that came out was a silver object shaped like a coin. A GIB mission disk!

'Hello, Agent Rock Star,' whispered the man behind the barbecue, giving Zac a small nod. 'I'm Agent Hot Dog.'

At that moment, Zac saw a Mike's Mobile Mowing van come swerving through the car park. It was one of those vans that came to your house to do your gardening – except this one had tinted windows.

Obviously, this was no ordinary gardening van.

It pulled up right behind Zac, and the doors flew open. Then he heard a familiar voice from inside.

'Get in, Zac!' said his brother Leon.

This could only mean one thing, thought Zac. *A new mission!*

CHAPTER 2

Zac climbed into the back of the van. Just as he'd thought, there wasn't a lawn mower or whipper snipper in sight. Instead, the walls were covered with wires, computer monitors and blinking lights.

Zac knew he was inside a GIB Mobile Technology Lab. His brother Leon, also known as Agent Tech Head, was standing at a small workbench. Leon was a computer whiz, science whiz and history whiz, all rolled up into one nerdy package. He didn't really go on missions. Instead he stayed behind, getting information to Zac, working on new gadgets, and somehow being uncool and useful at the same time.

The MTL doors swung shut, and the van started moving again. For a second Zac wondered who was driving. Then he remembered that Leon usually set the MTL to autopilot. That kept Leon's hands free for doing what he loved most – tinkering with gadgets.

Leon made a final adjustment to the new piece of GIB hardware he was working on, then looked up at Zac. 'Have you read your new mission yet?'

'I'm just about to,' said Zac, finishing off his sausage in bread. He wiped his hands on his pants and pulled out his SpyPad.

GIB agents never went anywhere without their SpyPad. It was the most useful spy gadget in the world – a super-charged tablet with a video phone, chemical analyser, laser, GPS and loads of other features.

Zac sat up on Leon's workbench, because he knew that annoyed him. He messaged his mum to let her know where he'd gone, and then slid the mission disk into his SpyPad.

CLASSIFIED

MISSION INITIATED: 2 P.M.

CURRENT TIME: 2.33 P.M.

The evil scientist Dr Drastic claims to have hatched a live dinosaur at the Bladesville BioDome. He will present the dinosaur to the International Science Council tomorrow afternoon.

However, GIB suspects that Drastic will attack the Council instead. He has planned something called Operation Extinct for 2 p.m. tomorrow.

YOUR MISSION: Confirm that the dinosaur is a fake. Find out what Operation Extinct is and stop it.

~ END ~

Zac looked up at Leon, his mouth hanging open. 'Dr Drastic is saying he's brought a dinosaur back to life? That's impossible!'

Zac knew that Dr Drastic was a brilliant scientist, but hatching a live dinosaur was a stretch even for him.

Leon shrugged. 'It's not entirely impossible,' he said. 'They died out millions of years ago, but some of them left behind fossils. If Dr Drastic found a really well-preserved fossil with bits of DNA, he maybe could have used the genetic sequence to …'

Zac could tell from the gleam in Leon's eye that he was going to explain exactly how Drastic might have done it. In precise detail. Possibly with diagrams.

'OK, OK,' Zac said quickly. He had to stop Leon now. 'I don't need to know the details. Just tell me whether you think it's a real dinosaur or not.'

Leon thought for a moment. 'Probably not, but you need to find out for sure. If it's a fake, then Drastic is obviously up to something. And we know he's wanted to take down the council for ages.'

Zac nodded. 'What kind of dinosaur is it supposed to be?'

'A Spinosaurus,' said Leon. 'A meat-eater, very dangerous – and even bigger than a T-Rex.'

'Bigger?' Zac asked.

Leon nodded. 'Longer, taller, probably faster – and with a head like a crocodile. But don't worry, it's only a baby-sized one.'

Leon shivered excitedly, and then glanced at the speedometer on the dashboard. 'I think we're going to need a bit more speed to get to Bladesville on time,' he added. 'Do you feel like driving?'

Zac grinned. 'Always,' he said, sitting down at the controls.

Whether the dinosaur was real or not, there was no time to waste when Dr Drastic was involved!

CHAPTER 3

Zac nudged the controls forward and gave the van an extra burst of speed. He'd been driving for a couple of hours, and the GPS screen on the dashboard showed that Bladesville was just up ahead.

A couple of raindrops splashed on the windscreen as dark clouds gathered in the sky. It looked like a storm was coming.

'OK,' said Leon, pointing to a section of the GPS screen. 'Drastic has been working out of the BioDome on the other side of the city, so we need to head there.'

Zac knew the BioDome was a special greenhouse where nerds like Leon studied different environments. It was weird to think of a garden growing in the middle of Bladesville's skyscrapers and dirty alleys.

Zac weaved the van through the noisy traffic on the outskirts of Bladesville. Even at the edge of the city, there were traffic jams everywhere.

He heard Leon's SpyPad beeping. He glanced back to see Leon frowning at his screen.

'GIB needs me back at HQ,' Leon said, looking up. 'And we'll never get anywhere in this traffic. You'd better stop the van and go the rest of the way on your own.'

Zac groaned. 'But the BioDome's on the other side of the city!'

Still, he pulled the van over to the side of the road and got up from the controls.

'I know,' said Leon, holding up a pair of thin, grey, metallic-looking straps. 'So it's a good thing I made you these!'

Leon wrapped the straps around Zac's hands. Each strap was wirelessly connected to a small suction pad.

'They're called SwingBands,' said Leon, sticking the suction pad to the back of

Zac's neck. 'Each band contains a tiny photonic cell and a super-strong magnet. The cell fires a focused beam that can magnetise a surface up to 200 metres away, and then –'

'Got it,' said Zac, rolling his eyes. 'It's like an invisible grappling hook that I can control with my hands.'

'Exactly!' said Leon. 'If you get your timing right, you can swing yourself through city streets, jungles, desert canyons – anywhere you can find a wall.'

'How do I activate them?' asked Zac.

'Follow me,' said Leon, pushing open the back door of the van. 'Now, hold out your hands carefully. And whatever you do, don't blink until I tell you.'

Zac sighed. He hated being told what to do by his nerdy older brother. But he was itching to see how these things worked.

Leon tapped the power stud on the back of each SwingBand. Then he stretched Zac's arm out as far as it could go.

'It's all controlled with your arm movements and brainwaves,' said Leon. 'The brain is just a big computer, after all. Point your palm where you want to go, hold your arm straight, then blink. It won't take you long to get into the, er, *swing* of it. OK?'

Zac ignored Leon's joke. He aimed his palm at the side of a building, stared at a window five floors up ... and then blinked.

WHOOSH!

Suddenly Zac was whisked from the back of the van and flew through the air – straight towards the side of the building!

'Swing yourself to the next one, before you go splat!' he heard Leon yell from the ground.

Zac threw his arm toward a building on the other side of the road – ten floors up this time.

He fixed his eyes on where he wanted to go, blinked, and –

WHOOSH!

He changed direction just before he smashed into the side of the building.

Aim, blink …

WHOOSH! WHOOSH!

Zac was swinging between buildings, fifteen floors up now. Cars and trucks inched along the road below, totally unaware of the secret agent zipping through the air above them like Spiderman.

Then Zac remembered something.

How in the world do I STOP these things?

 **BEEP-BEEP!**

Zac's SpyPad was beeping. It was probably Leon calling. Zac couldn't reach the SpyPad, so he activated the hands-free control.

'Authorise SpyPad: Agent Rock Star,' he shouted. 'Open message!'

'Zac, it's Leon!' came a voice from the SpyPad. 'I forgot to tell you two things! One, press the stud on the back of the SwingBands to power them down. Two, don't use them the whole way to the BioDome – you should save some power for later!'

Zac groaned. 'Now he tells me!'

CHAPTER

Zac was hurtling straight towards an apartment block. *I guess I should switch off the SwingBands soon,* he thought. *But how do I make a safe landing?*

Then Zac noticed a set of metal fire escape steps on the side of the apartments. On instinct, Zac flicked off his SwingBands and threw himself at the railing – a split second before he slammed into the wall!

I am awesome, thought Zac. Then he realised he was still dangling on the edge of the fire escape – 15 floors up!

Zac used all his strength to pull himself over the railing and onto the steps.

Now that he'd stopped flying through the air, Zac got his breath back and checked the time on his SpyPad. It was 7 p.m.

Better get a move on, thought Zac. He climbed down the fire escape steps and jumped to the ground. He found himself in a dark alley, next to an overflowing rubbish bin. Zac wrinkled his nose. *Why has today been so smelly?*

He turned to head out of the laneway.

Then he heard a rumble of thunder. Moments later, heavy rain began falling from the sky. Lightning flickered around the tops of skyscrapers, and Zac could feel the crackle of electricity in the air.

Oh great, he thought. *An electrical storm. I'll have to wait this one out.*

Zac ducked under a ledge, hoping to stay there until the rain eased up. But instead, the downpour got so bad that Zac could barely see.

Great, he thought, shivering. *Standing around under a fire escape, with nothing but a smelly bin for company!*

Then Zac remembered he was carrying a SafeCrate, one of GIB's latest inventions.

He reached into his pocket and pulled out a small grey object with dimples all over it like a golf ball.

Zac ducked back into the alley. He squeezed the SafeCrate three times and put it on the ground behind the dumpster, resting it flat on one of the dimples.

The ball got bigger and bigger until it came up to Zac's hip. Zac reached out and pressed three of the dimples in a special order know only to GIB agents.

A hatch opened in the side of the sphere. Zac crawled inside and shut the door. The inside of the ball was small, but the walls were fitted with inflatable padding for comfort.

At least Zac would stay warm and dry for a while. The only problem was that he'd be bored out of his brain!

Zac got out his SpyPad. A good spy always used his time wisely. Even though what Zac really wanted to do was load up a game of *Crazy Cannibal Cavemen*, he decided to do some dinosaur research instead. There was still a chance that Drastic's dinosaur was real, after all.

Zac set the SpyPad to Research Mode and typed in 'Spinosaurus'.

An article came up from GIBpedia, the GIB information database. Zac scrolled through pages and pages of text, looking for useful information. He couldn't help noticing that most of the info had been added by a certain Agent Tech Head.

My brother is such a nerd, thought Zac, yawning.

According to the main page, the Spinosaurus had died out about 100 million years ago. One hundred million years!

Zac wondered sleepily what it would be like to see a real live Spinosaurus. He still couldn't believe Dr Drastic had managed to create a whole dinosaur – even a baby one – just from some old fossil.

Zac scrolled through a few more pages. He yawned again. He'd already done a lot of research.

I should probably shut my eyes for a moment,

he told himself as the rain pelted down on the SafeCrate. *I need to be alert in case Drastic's dinosaur is real. I don't want to end up being its lunch!*

When Zac opened his eyes a few hours later, the first thing he noticed was the silence. The rain had stopped pounding down.

Zac tried to stretch a bit, but it was pretty cramped inside the SafeCrate. Then he glanced at the SpyPad.

It was 9 a.m. the next day. He'd slept for way too long, and now there were only five hours left to complete his mission!

Oh no, he thought with a groan. *Leon's going to kill me!*

Zac slipped out of the SafeCrate and pressed another combination of buttons to shrink it down to size.

Then he put it back in his pocket and started racing on foot through the busy streets of Bladesville.

It took Zac more than an hour to reach Dr Drastic's BioDome on the other side of the city.

He slowed down to a jog when he saw it up ahead, surrounded by white and silver skyscrapers.

It was a massive glass dome with a sliding metallic door on one side. Through the glass, Zac could see a lush, colourful jungle.

Tourists were making their way inside. Zac joined the end of the line, using his spy skills to blend in with one of the families. For all Zac knew, Dr Drastic could be watching his every move. The line took forever to get to the ticket counter.

As Zac shuffled closer, he saw a sign near the entrance:

BLADESVILLE BIODOME
OPEN TO THE PUBLIC
9 a.m. – 1 p.m.
CHILDREN ADMITTED FREE

It's weird that Drastic doesn't keep the BioDome open all day, Zac thought. *He'd make more money from the Spinosaurus if he did.*

Zac finally made it into the BioDome and slipped off into the crowd.

He'd been in real jungles before, and if he didn't know better he'd think he was in one now. The air was hot, and the dome was filled with snaking vines, strange-looking flowers and thick trees.

There was an excited crowd gathering around a small wire fence nearby.

Zac was just wondering what they were looking at when he heard a squawking, croaking noise.

He peered through the crowd, trying

to work out where the bizarre sound was coming from.

And then he saw it.

Dr Drastic's baby dinosaur!

CHAPTER 5

Zac's mouth dropped open.

The spinosaurus was taller than Zac. *That's hardly baby-sized,* he thought. Its head was shaped like a crocodile's, just like Leon had said, and it had a long mouth full of sharp teeth.

The creature stood on a pair of thick legs, with a powerful-looking tail behind.

Sticking out the front of its body were two stubby arms, each ending in a set of long, curved claws. Along its spine was a sharp fin.

Zac was impressed. It certainly looked like a real dinosaur, not that he'd ever seen one before. Still, he had a nagging feeling that something wasn't right. But what?

One of the staff from the BioDome was standing by, keeping a close eye on the creature and making sure no-one tried to get over the fence. Every now and then the spinosaurus let out another weird squawk, making everyone gasp.

Zac edged closer to the fence for a better look. A TV crew was putting cameras and spotlights and sound equipment into position around the dinosaur.

Zac recognised the logo on the side of the cameras. This crew was from *Creepy Creatures*, Leon's favourite TV show! Zac knew his brother would be super jealous.

SPINOSAURUS SPECIAL!

CREEPY CREATURES

He turned his attention back to the baby spinosaurus. He watched closely as it bared its teeth and squawked again. It seemed to shudder ever so slightly when it moved its head.

It was as though the spinosaurus was somehow almost … mechanical.

Suddenly, someone shoved a microphone in Zac's face. All the *Creepy Creatures* cameras swung in his direction.

'So, little boy,' said the man holding the microphone, 'are you a big fan of dinosaurs? Have you come to see the baby spinosaurus?'

Zac fought to control his anger. *Little boy?* But at the same time, his spy senses told him not to blow his cover. He couldn't risk being the centre of attention. He had to get that camera off him!

'Um, no,' he mumbled, looking down at his feet. 'I'm here because I really like, um … flowers.'

The presenter frowned, shrugged and moved on. 'What about you, little girl?' Zac heard him say. 'Frightened by the spinosaurus?'

Phew! Zac knew there was something off about the dinosaur, and he needed to keep moving if he was going to find Drastic. Operation Extinct was supposed to happen in just a few hours!

Zac walked away from the crowd and crept into the thick jungle. This whole place was a sort of like a laboratory – so where were all the scientists? They didn't seem to be inside the BioDome. Maybe they were underneath it.

And if so, that's probably where Dr Drastic was, too.

Zac snooped around, looking for any kind of hidden exit or tunnel. Soon he saw a hatch in the ground. He crept over and lifted the door open. Below was a ladder leading down into darkness.

Zac checked his SpyPad again. It was now 11.33 a.m. Less than two and a half hours to go. No time to lose!

Zac scurried down the ladder, which took him to a large room. There was a big roller door at one end and a doorway across the room.

Zac was about to sneak over when the roller door clanked open, revealing a ramp on the other side. He was clearly in some kind of delivery bay.

Two trucks backed down the ramp and into the bay. Zac ducked out of sight as the trucks came to a halt and men in overalls got out.

Zac noticed hundreds of tyre marks leading in and out of the bay. *So whatever these trucks are delivering,* he thought, *they're coming here all the time.*

Then Zac had a brainwave. Maybe they were delivering food for the spinosaurus! If it was a real dinosaur, it would need huge amounts of meat every day.

But the men weren't unloading meat. From one of the trucks, the men were carrying out little boxes with wires and knobs coming out of them.

They're not boxes, realised Zac. *They're batteries.* Suddenly he knew what was going on. The baby spinosaurus was obviously battery-powered – which meant it was a fake!

Zac felt a twinge of disappointment. *Leon will be upset,* he thought.

From the other truck, the men hooked up a hose and started pumping something into the ground. Zac sniffed the air. It smelt like when his mum filled the car up at the service station. Petrol!

Weird, thought Zac. *Why would Drastic need that much petrol?* He doubted that the spinosaurus was battery *and* petrol-powered.

The men climbed into the trucks. As the vehicles reversed up the ramp, BioDome staff dressed in white lab coats came in. They loaded the batteries onto trolleys and carted them out the door.

Zac counted to 20, then sprinted across the bay and slipped through after them.

The baby spinosaurus was fake, so Drastic obviously wasn't going to present his research to the International Science Council.

Maybe the petrol is part of Operation Extinct,

Zac realised. *What if Drastic is planning to drive a really big vehicle down to the Science Council HQ in Bladesville Central?*

Who knew what kind of crazy war machine Drastic could dream up?

I have to stop him! thought Zac.

Though the door, Zac found himself in a maze of white corridors.

Every so often, there was a door marked **STAFF ONLY** or **HAZARDOUS WASTE** or **LAB STORAGE**.

But Zac didn't have time to check every door. He had to follow his spy senses – and his senses told him he was getting closer and closer to Dr Drastic.

Suddenly, he heard a familiar voice from

behind him. 'Hello, Agent Rock Star.'

Zac spun around. As usual, his spy senses were right.

'Well, well,' sneered Dr Drastic. 'I wish I could say it was nice to see you again!'

CHAPTER

Dr Drastic was wearing a white lab coat, like the other BioDome staff, and had a name-tag pinned to his chest. There were two huge goons in grey jumpsuits behind him.

Dr Drastic stared at Zac with his icy blue eyes. Zac knew that one of those eyes was made of glass. It always creeped him out, but Zac never let it show.

'Congratulations on your fake baby dinosaur,' said Zac. 'Looks like it's inherited your good looks.'

Dr Drastic ignored him. 'I spotted you snooping around upstairs. I had the TV cameras bugged, you see. They're totally under my control – like everything in the BioDome. Including you!'

Zac only got as far as saying, 'You don't control me –' when Dr Drastic reached inside his lab coat and whipped out a strange device. It looked like a spray bottle of some kind.

Dr Drastic pointed the device at Zac and pulled a trigger on the handle.

Liquid shot from the nozzle straight at Zac!

SPLUUUURRT!

Before he could leap out of the way, Zac felt the thick spray hit his hands and face. He went to wipe the liquid away – then suddenly realised he couldn't move.

'A temporary muscle-constricting solution,' said Dr Drastic. 'I extracted it from a tropical plant that's been extinct for millions of years. The scientists here at the BioDome reconstructed its genetic sequence – with the help of my immense genius, of course.'

Zac went to talk, but even his jaw and tongue and facial muscles were stuck.

He was totally paralysed!

Dr Drastic clicked his fingers. Zac watched helplessly as the two goons stepped forward and picked him up. They hoisted Zac onto their shoulders and carted him down the winding maze of corridors.

Zac couldn't see where they were taking him. All he could do was stare up at the roof, and try to memorise the route they were following. He felt like he'd been turned into a statue.

Eventually he heard Dr Drastic's voice. 'Put him down over there.'

They'd left the twisting corridors and

were in a darker, more shadowy section of the complex. The henchmen planted Zac on his feet and leant him against a trolley.

They were inside what could only have been Dr Drastic's personal laboratory.

Zac had lost count of the number of times he'd been inside one of Drastic's labs. The evil scientist set them up everywhere, in volcanoes and diamond mines and underwater caves.

From the corner of his eye, Zac saw the two goons leave. Meanwhile, Dr Drastic gestured around the lab. He was holding some sort of remote control.

'Here's where it begins – Operation Extinct!' Dr Drastic boomed.

Then he gave Zac a concerned look. 'What's that, Rock Star? I can't quite hear you. It sounds like you're trying to tell me what a genius I am.'

Zac tried desperately to shake movement back into his muscles. The best he could do was wriggle his toes. Drastic had said the poison was temporary – so was it slowly wearing off?

Zac concentrated hard, trying to move a little more, and a little more, while Drastic chattered away.

'Well, you'd be right, I am a genius!' Dr Drastic grinned. 'And if you want further proof …'

Drastic stabbed a button on his remote,

and a huge rectangular section of the laboratory floor slid away.

The smell of petrol hit Zac's nostrils. He saw steam rising up from the hole in the floor and heard a loud mechanical clanking from below.

If Zac hadn't been paralysed, his mouth would have dropped open for the second time that day. Because as the floor opened up, he realised that Drastic's baby spinosaurus had just been practice.

In the area beneath the floor, Drastic had built the biggest monster Zac had ever seen. It was a massive mechanical dinosaur, at least twenty times bigger than the baby spinosaurus upstairs.

So that's why Drastic needed all that petrol,
Zac gulped.

CHAPTER 7

'This is my masterpiece – the Robosaur!'
crowed Dr Drastic. 'Remote-controlled
and everything. Look, I can even make it
blink!'

He pointed the remote at the enormous
robosaur and clicked a button. Zac watched
as sheets of metal folded over its glowing
red LED eyes, and then opened again.

'It's so realistic,' bragged Dr Drastic. 'It mimics the act of blinking in a very natural way.'

Then the robosaur opened its mouth, and Zac got an all-too-clear glimpse of the jagged metal spikes Dr Drastic had used for its teeth.

Zac could still smell the stench of petrol, and he knew it must have an enormous engine somewhere inside.

I guess battery power wouldn't be enough for a robot dinosaur that big, he thought.

Zac tried to move his arms again. Movement had returned to his fingers, and he could turn his eyes from side to side.

The poison was wearing off, but would

it wear off fast enough for Zac to stop whatever Dr Drastic was planning? If he managed to stretch his arm out, he could use his SwingBands. But his hands were still pinned to his sides.

'I know you've guessed the truth about my baby dinosaur upstairs,' Dr Drastic was sneering. 'But not the whole truth. My experiment did work a little bit – I used the DNA sequence to research what a spinosaurus would look like, right down to the smallest detail. And then I hired the best animatronic makers in the business!'

Zac summoned all his energy. He still couldn't work his arms and legs, but at last he was able to get his jaw moving.

'Nothing – but – a fake,' Zac said through clenched teeth. 'Even Leon – can build – a robot!' Every word was a massive effort.

'You're missing the point, Rock Star,' ranted Drastic. 'I could have created the whole dinosaur out of living tissue, but the Science Council idiots wouldn't give me more money! They said it wasn't possible to bring a dinosaur back to life. Well, at two o'clock precisely, they're going to meet one face-to-face!'

So that's Operation Extinct, thought Zac. He had to keep this crazy scientist talking.

'I – suppose – you're going to let – that big thing – eat me?' he said.

'Don't be stupid,' snarled Dr Drastic, strolling over to a corner of the lab. He wheeled a turbo scooter out from behind a bench.

'This big thing, as you call it, is far more important than that. Together, we're going to tear down the Science Council Headquarters in Bladesville! Maybe *then* they'll reconsider funding my research!'

Yeah, sure, thought Zac. *They'll be so happy about you tearing their building down that they'll want to give you money, YOU CRAZY OLD MAN!*

Zac wanted to laugh, but it was no joke. People could get hurt. There were even GIB agents working undercover at the International Science Council, keeping an eye on all the latest scientific developments.

Dr Drastic had to be stopped!

'Anyway,' shouted Dr Drastic, stepping onto the turbo scooter, 'you're right about one thing.' He pressed a button on his remote control. 'You *are* going to be eaten!'

Zac heard a noise above him. He could move his neck muscles just enough to see three long green shapes slowly descending from the roof towards him.

At first he thought they were snakes. Then, to his relief, he realised they were jungle vines.

'Common liana crossed with a giant Venus flytrap,' shouted Dr Drastic, laughing madly. 'In other words, meat-eating vines! And they're attracted to heat, so you're a goner. So long, Agent Rock Star!'

Zac's relief suddenly vanished. The vines may as *well* have been snakes!

Drastic took his scooter into a small elevator in the wall of the lab, cackling madly as the doors slid shut.

Zac guessed that Drastic would ride alongside the robosaur, controlling it by remote all the way to the Science Council HQ.

But Zac had other problems to deal

with first. He was now alone in the lab with the meat-eating vines. And he still couldn't move his body!

CHAPTER 8

The hungry vines snaked closer and closer toward him. Zac could see their snapping, clam-like mouths and pointy, needle-sharp teeth ...

Suddenly, Zac remembered he'd been fitted with GIB issue MediMolars – fake teeth loaded with instant medication. All you had to do was prod the fake tooth three times with your tongue to open the tooth and release the medication. It would help Zac move again.

If only he'd remembered sooner! He felt like slapping himself in the head, except he was still paralysed.

Zac had two MediMolars. They were fitted right at the back of his bottom teeth, one on each side. One released an instant anti-toxin, designed to flush any poison from an agent's system.

The other MediMolar released an amnesia serum. If you were caught, it would make you temporarily forget everything you know – so you couldn't reveal GIB secrets under pressure.

The problem was, Zac couldn't quite remember which tooth did which. He was pretty sure it was the left tooth, but not 100 per cent …

If I accidentally release the amnesia serum, I'll forget to open the other MediMolar, thought Zac. *I'll get eaten by the vines for sure!*

Zac decided to trust his gut instinct. He concentrated on using his tongue to prod the left MediMolar, just as the vines slithered down towards his head.

The MediMolar broke open, and Zac felt the medication flow through his body.

He flexed one hand, then the other. He could move! He raced out of the lab, just as the heat-seeking vines snapped down right where he'd been standing. He checked the time on his SpyPad as he ran.

It was 12.45 p.m. In just over an hour, Dr Drastic and his robosaur would be tearing down the International Science Council building.

Zac focused on the route he'd memorised when Dr Drastic's henchmen had carried him to the lab. When he was sure he had it clearly in his head, he sprinted off down the maze of corridors.

It took him almost 45 minutes, but eventually Zac bolted through the door into the delivery bay. He ran over to the ladder that led to the surface of the

BioDome and started climbing.

When he reached the top, he forced the door open and hauled himself up into the hot, dense jungle.

Zac fought his way through the vegetation towards the open spaces near the main door. When he came out, he was surprised to see that the crowds had gone. The place was empty.

Just as Zac remembered that the BioDome was closed to the public at one o'clock … three long green vines lashed out at him from the jungle!

More of Dr Drastic's meat-eating plants! Zac ducked and rolled, expertly dodging the vines' attack, then leapt to his feet and spun around.

This time he was ready. He reached into the pocket of his cargo pants and pulled out a spiky pinecone-shaped gadget with a black pin on the end.

It was an experimental GIB PhotoSynth Grenade. Guaranteed to distract people and animals with a burst of concentrated, artificial sunlight.

The meat-eating vines swung through the air for a moment, got a fix on Zac again, and flexed forward on their long, snake-like bodies.

Zac twisted the black pin on the gadget, setting the grenade's timer to five seconds. Then he pulled the pin and hurled the

grenade at the meat-eating vines.

FWOOOOSH!

There was a white flash. The vines stopped and reared up like cobras. They swayed in the air, dazzled by the light – giving Zac just enough time to slip away.

Zac pushed further and further through the jungle. He knew the main door was close. And then –

THUD!

Zac had run straight into something scaly and solid. The impact knocked him on his back.

He looked up to see the giant baby spinosaurus standing above him. Unlike Zac, the dinosaur had managed to remain on its feet. It had hardly budged when Zac ran into it.

Zac backed away, trying not to panic. It was just a robot, but Drastic had probably programmed it with all the speed and hunting skills of a real spinosaurus.

And it also happened to be blocking the only door to the outside.

CHAPTER 9

Zac ran through a list of tactics in his mind. *I can't outrun it,* he thought. Could he trick it? Offer it some instant SpyFood? Confuse it with a blast of Axe Grinder from his music collection?

Think, Zac! he told himself.

And then he realised something. The robot spinosaurus wasn't moving *at all*.

Of course, thought Zac, as he got to his feet. If the baby spinosaurus was battery-powered, Drastic would switch it off when no-one was around.

Relieved, Zac checked the time. It was 1.37 p.m. Just 22 minutes left to save the day!

He raced through the main doors of the BioDome and out into the streets of Bladesville. In the distance he could hear yelling, and hundreds of car horns honking and blaring. It sounded to Zac like Drastic had taken his giant robosaur to the street.

As Zac ran, a plan popped into his head. He switched on his SwingBands, hoping madly that they still had power in them.

He focused on a building up ahead and blinked. An instant later, he was suddenly pulled through the air.

WHOOSH!

Zac swung from building to building, following the trail of damage Dr Drastic and his robosaur had left behind.

Aim, blink,

WHOOSH!

Aim, blink,

WHOOSH!

Zac wondered if he'd get a warning when the SwingBands' power was running out. Leon was useless at adding important features like that.

Zac looked down as he rushed past

the street below. There were squashed vehicles everywhere. Luckily it looked like everyone had got out and run for cover when they'd seen the giant metal monster coming.

Dr Drastic would be heading straight for Bladesville Central. Zac was sure to catch sight of him any moment now … *There!*

Up ahead, Zac saw the robot dinosaur stomping straight towards the International Science Council building. He could just make out Dr Drastic riding alongside on his turbo scooter.

The robosaur was enormous. Along its spine was the same sort of fin the baby spinosaurus had on its back, except the robot dinosaur's fin was made of thin, flexible metal. Drastic clearly hadn't bothered to make this one look completely real.

Zac had to bring down the robosaur before it reached the Council's building and really went crazy. He only had one plan, and he just had to hope it worked ...

Zac swung closer and closer, and when he was near enough, he pointed his hand at the robosaur's back and blinked.

ZAP! SHOOOOONK!

The SwingBands locked him on. Zac was flying straight towards the robosaur!

Just before he slammed into the

creature's metal body, Zac reached out and grabbed hold of the fin. He clung tight to the flexible sheet of metal, which bent and wobbled as the robosaur crunched its way into Main Square.

Luckily, Drastic hadn't seen him yet.

Zac used his hands to edge himself closer to the robosaur's head. Soon he was at the base of its neck. Zac let go of the fin, balanced himself on his hands and feet, then pulled himself up towards the head.

Zac was very, very careful not to blink – his SwingBands were still powered on and he didn't want to go flying off the robosaur before he could stop it.

Down on the ground, Dr Drastic

whooped with delight, unaware that Zac was on the robosaur.

Zac slowly pulled the SwingBands from his hands and unpeeled the suction pad from the back of his neck. He reached out to the head of the robosaur – but at that exact moment, the crazy scientist looked up and saw Zac!

'Noooooo!' he screamed.

Zac moved quickly, strapping the SwingBands onto the robosaur's head and planting the suction pad just near the glowing LED eyes. He desperately hoped his plan would work!

Dr Drastic sneered. 'I know what you're trying to do, Rock Star,' he yelled.

'You think you can turn off its Cybernetic brain! Well, forget it – you'll never get through that metal plating!'

'You'll see,' smiled Zac. 'Whoops, better watch out!'

Zac pointed ahead. The robot dinosaur was about to crash into a huge flashing billboard. Dr Drastic panicked and fumbled with his remote control – madly pressing buttons as he tried to steer the robot dinosaur away from the billboard.

Zac clung to the creature's neck. He had to jump off, because any second now, the robosaur was going to blink.

And when he did –

WHOOOOOOSH!

Suddenly Zac felt the robosaur get whisked upwards. The giant mechanical monster had blinked, and locked the SwingBands onto a nearby building – and now it was flying through the air!

CHAPTER 10

Gotta go, thought Zac. Taking a deep breath, he flung himself off the robosaur ...

... And then he was flying through the air without SwingBands. And no way to land safely!

Suddenly Zac had an idea.

He pulled the SafeCrate from his pocket and expanded it to full size as he fell.

With just seconds before he slammed into the ground, Zac pulled himself inside the SafeCrate and slammed the door shut.

He pressed his hands and feet against the walls as —

BOING!!!!!

The SafeCrate hit the ground. Zac stretched out like a starfish, trying to stay limp as the impact sent shockwaves through his body.

He felt the SafeCrate bounce, bounce, bounce — and then gently roll to a stop.

Zac leapt out of the SafeCrate as fast as he could. He needed to see what had happened!

The whole of Main Square was buzzing

with choppers, but the giant robosaur was nowhere to be found.

Then Zac saw it – the smoking, mangled wreck of the robot dinosaur, wedged in an alley between two buildings.

But where was Dr Drastic? He was gone!

That lousy scientist! thought Zac, clenching his fists.

He was glad everyone was safe from the robosaur, but he was annoyed that Drastic had gotten away.

One of the GIB choppers landed in the middle of Main Square, and Leon jumped out.

'Zac!' he called. 'We've been trying to

get you on your SpyPad!'

'Sorry, Leon,' said Zac. 'I was a bit busy bringing down a monster robosaur!'

'I know,' said Leon. 'We saw the whole thing. Quick thinking with the SwingBands, by the way. I'm amazed they worked on the robosaur – they're only designed for human brains.'

'Well,' said Zac smugly, 'the brain *is* just a big computer, after all.'

Leon nodded. 'That is so right.'

Zac rolled his eyes. 'Hey, by the way – how are you going to cover up a giant robot dinosaur attacking Bladesville?'

'Don't worry, GIB has it sorted,' Leon said. 'Our undercover agents are telling the papers that it's a runaway prop from the new *Killer Robots* movie.'

Zac laughed. People would believe anything! Just then, he felt his SpyPad vibrating. He had an incoming message from his mum.

Good work on Operation Extinct, said the message. *But don't forget you've got Operation Compost when you get home!*

~ MISSION CHECKLIST ~
How many have you read?

FOSSIL FURY
H. I. LARRY

FROZEN FEAR
H. I. LARRY

SHOCK MUSIC
H. I. LARRY

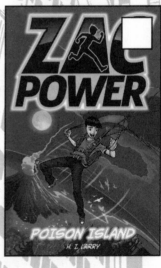

POISON ISLAND
H. I. LARRY